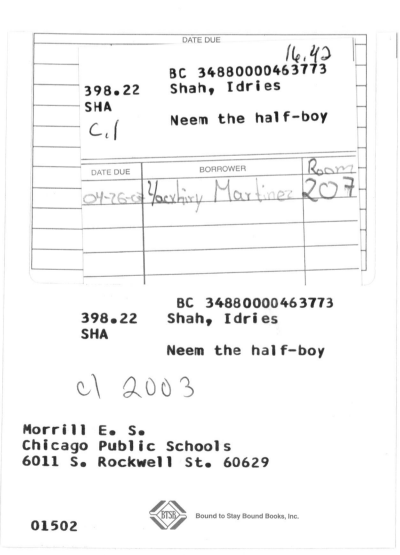

First Edition

HOOPOE

Published by Hoopoe Books,
a division of The Institute for the Study of Human Knowledge

ISBN: 1-883536-10-3
Library of Congress Cataloging-in-Publication Data

Shah, Idries, 1924-
       Neem the half-boy / by Idries Shah; illustrated by Robert Revels
& Midori Mori.
                          p.   cm.
       Summary: Because she does not faithfully follow the instructions
of Arif the Wise Man, the Queen of Hich-Hich gives birth to a half-boy,
who grows up to be very clever and confronts a dragon in an effort to
become whole.
       ISBN 1-883536-10-3 (hard)
       [1. Fairy tales. 2. Folklore.] I. Revels, Robert, ill.
       II. Mori, Midori, ill. III Title.
       PZ8.S336Ne   1997

       398.22--dc21
       [E]
                                                              97-6321
                                                              CIP
                                                                 AC

Printed in China through Palace Press International.

NEEM THE HALF-BOY

BY IDRIES SHAH

HOOPOE BOOKS
BOSTON

Once upon a time, when flies flew backwards and the sun was cool, there was a country called Hich-Hich, which means "nothing at all."

This country had a king, and it also had a queen.

Now the queen wanted to have a little boy
for a son because she didn't have one.

"How can I get a little boy?" she asked the
king.

"I don't know, I'm sure," the king replied.

So the queen asked all the people, and they said,
    "We are very sorry, but we can't tell Your Majesty how to get
a little boy."
    (They called her "Your Majesty" because you always call
queens — and kings too — Your Majesty.)

So the queen asked the fairies, and they said,
"We could go and ask Arif the Wise Man."
The wise man was a very clever man, and he knew everything.
So the fairies went to the place where Arif the Wise Man lived, and they said to him,
"We are the fairies from the country of Hich-Hich. That country has a queen, and she wants a little boy, but she doesn't know how to get one."
"I'll tell you how the queen can have a little boy for a son," said Arif the Wise Man, with a smile.

And he picked up an apple,
and he gave it to the fairies, saying,
"Give this apple to the queen
and tell her to eat it. If she eats it,
she will have a little boy."

So the fairies took the apple and
flew back to the queen.

"Your Majesty, we have been to
see the wise man, Arif, who knows
everything," they told her, "and he
says that you should eat this apple.
If you eat it, you will have a little
boy for a son."

The queen was very pleased. She started to eat the apple, but before she had finished it, she forgot how important it was and started thinking about something else. And she dropped the apple, only half eaten.

And she did have a little boy.
But, because she had eaten only half of
the apple, the boy she had was a half-boy.

He had one eye and one ear, one arm
and one leg, and he hopped wherever
he went.

The queen called him Prince Neem,
because "neem" means "half" in
the language of that country.

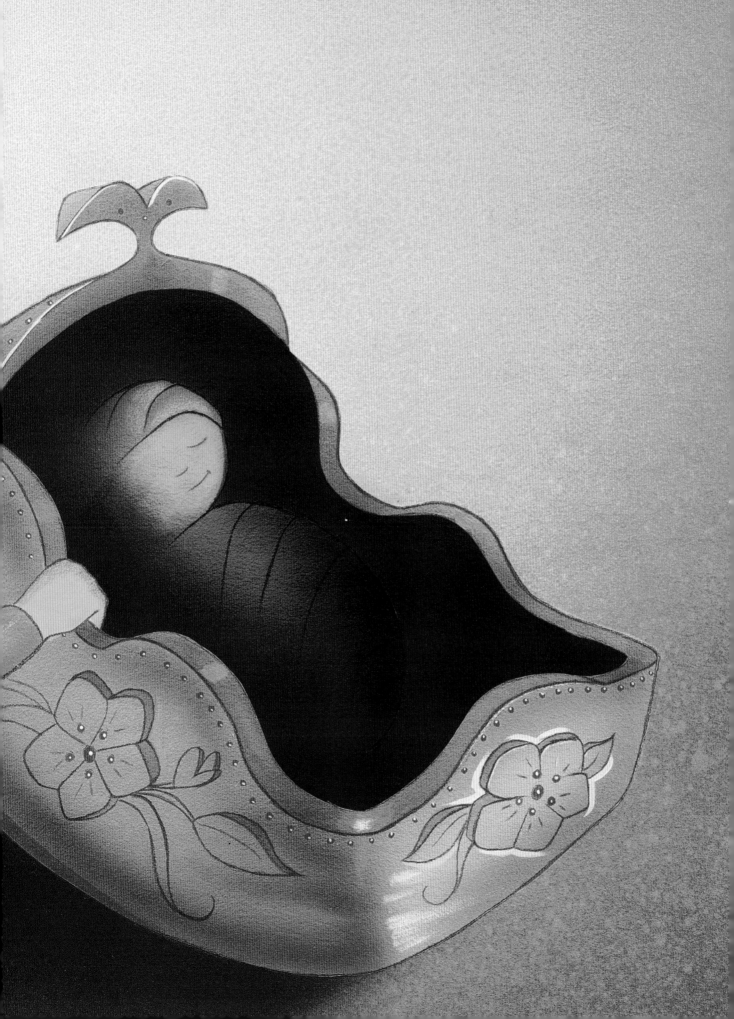

As he grew bigger, Prince Neem went everywhere on a horse. As a half-boy, he could get around better on a horse, because he didn't have to hop.

He became very clever at riding his horse, and he grew to be a very clever little boy in every way.

But he got bored with being a half-boy, and he used
to say, "I would like to be a whole boy. How can I
become a whole boy?"

And the queen would answer, "I'm sure I don't know."

And the king would say, "I have no idea at all."

And the fairies, when they came to hear about it, said,

"Perhaps we should go and ask the wise man, who knows every-thing, how Prince Neem can become a whole boy."

So the fairies flew through the air to the place where Arif the Wise Man lived, and they said to him,

"We are the fairies who came to see you about the Queen of Hich-Hich who wanted a little boy, but he is only a half-boy, and he wants to be a whole boy. Can you help him?"

And Arif the Wise Man sighed and said, "The queen ate only half the apple. That is why she had only a half-boy. But, since that was so long ago, she cannot eat the other half. It must have gone bad by now."

"Well, is there anything that Neem, the half-boy, can do to become a whole boy?" asked the fairies.

"Tell Neem, the half-boy, that he can go to see Taneen, the fire-breathing dragon. He lives in a cave and is annoying everyone around by blowing fire all over them. The half-boy will find a special, wonderful medicine in Taneen's cave. If he drinks it, he will become a whole boy. Go and tell him that," said Arif the Wise Man.

So the fairies flew into the air, and they didn't stop flying until they came to the palace where the king and the queen and Neem, the half-boy, lived.

When they got there, they found Prince Neem and said to him,
"We have been to see Arif the Wise Man, who is very clever and knows
everything. He told us to tell you that you must drive out Taneen the
Dragon, who is annoying the people. In the back of his cave you will find
the special, wonderful medicine which will make you into a whole boy."

Prince Neem thanked the fairies, got on his horse, and trotted it to the cave where Taneen the Dragon was sitting, breathing fire all over the place.

"Now I am going to drive you out, Dragon!" cried Prince Neem to Taneen.

"But why should you?" asked Taneen.

And Prince Neem said, "I am going to drive you away because you keep breathing fire all over people and they don't like it."

"I must breathe fire because I have to cook my food. If I had a stove to do my cooking on, I wouldn't have to do it," replied Taneen sadly.

"I could give you a stove to do your cooking on. But I must still drive you out," said the prince, and the dragon replied,

"Why should you, if I stopped breathing fire over people?"

"I would have to get you to go because you have got a special, wonderful medicine in the back of your cave. If I drink it I can become a whole boy, and I want to be a whole boy very much," said Neem.

"But I could give you the medicine, so that you would not have to drive me away to get it. You could drink it, and you would become a whole boy. Then you could go and get me a stove, and I would be able to do my cooking, and I wouldn't have to blow fire all over people!" said the dragon.

So Neem waited while the dragon went into the back of his
cave. Presently Taneen came back with a bottle of the special,
wonderful medicine.
 Prince Neem drank it all down,

and in less time than it takes
to tell, he grew another arm,
another side, another leg, another
ear and everything.

He had become a whole boy!
And he was very, very pleased.

He got on his horse and rode quickly back to the palace at
Hich-Hich. There he fetched a cooking-stove and took it back
to Taneen.

And after that Taneen the Dragon lived quietly in his cave,
and never blew fire over anyone again, and all the people were
very happy.

From then on, Neem, the half-boy, was called Kull, which means "the whole-boy" in the language of Hich-Hich.

It would have been silly of him to be called a half-boy when he was a whole one, wouldn't it?

And everyone lived happily for evermore.

Other Books by Idries Shah

γ